# Usborne Sticker Atlas of the World

Fiona Patchett and Alice Pearcey
Illustrated by Tim Benton

Designed by Sarah Cronin,
Stephen Moncrieff and Lucy Owen

Edited by Gillian Doherty
Consultant: Zoë Tomlinson

# Contents

4 Africa

6 Asia

8 North and Central America

10 South America

12 The Middle East

13 Australasia

14 Europe

16 Flags of the world

22 World records

24 Index and checklist

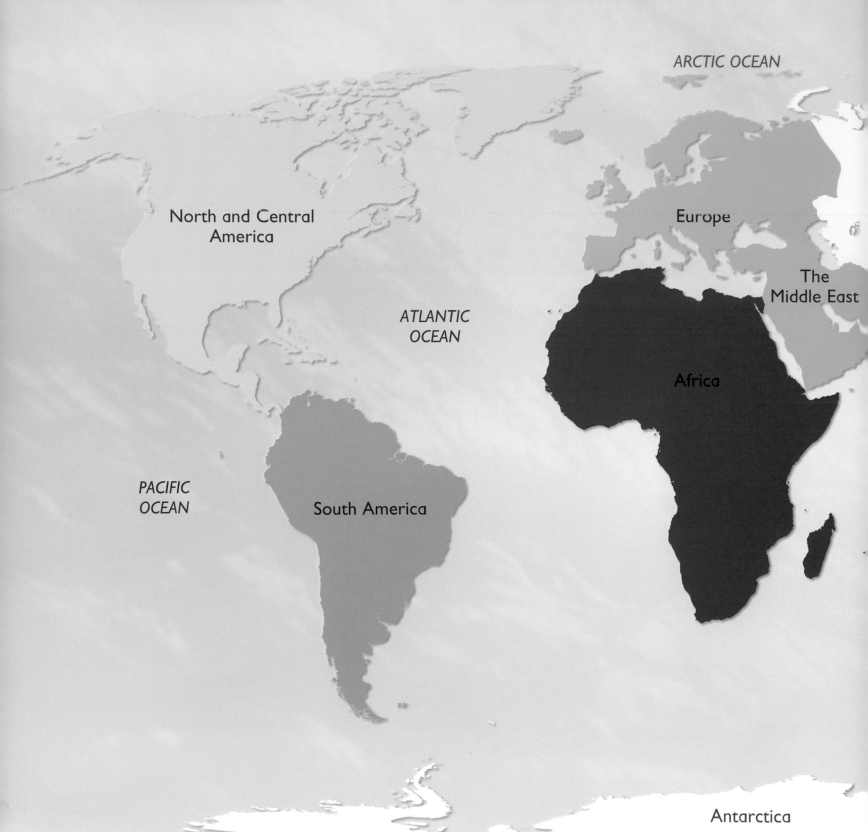

ARCTIC OCEAN

North and Central America

Europe

The Middle East

ATLANTIC OCEAN

Africa

PACIFIC OCEAN

South America

Antarctica

Asia

PACIFIC
OCEAN

INDIAN
OCEAN

Australasia

## How to use this book

There are more than 140 stickers in this book, showing some of the most famous sights in the world, including the Great Wall of China and Niagara Falls. To find out where each one is, try to match the stickers in the middle of the book to the black and white drawings on the maps.

The stickers are numbered, so you can tell which map they go on. A list on each map tells you the names of the sights, and there's a checklist at the back of the book to help you.

## Using the maps

The shading on the maps on pages 4–15 shows what the land is like in different places. This key explains what the shading and the lines on the maps represent.

- Forests
- Deserts
- Mountains
- Tundra
- Ice and snow
- Other (grassland, farmland and cities)
- Seas and oceans
- Lakes
- Rivers
- Country boundaries
- Country boundaries through water

## World maps

Every map in this book has a small world map next to it. The area shaded red shows you which part of the world is shown on the big map.

This is the world map that goes with the big map of South America on pages 10–11.

# Africa

Mediterranean Sea

MOROCCO

Madeira (Portugal)

TUNISIA

Canary Islands (Spain)

ALGERIA

LIBYA

WESTERN SAHARA (Morocco)

MALI

NIGER

MAURITANIA

CAPE VERDE

CH

SENEGAL

THE GAMBIA

BURKINA FASO

GUINEA-BISSAU

GUINEA

GHANA

BENIN

TOGO

NIGERIA

SIERRA LEONE

IVORY COAST

LIBERIA

*ATLANTIC OCEAN*

CAMEROON

EQUATORIAL GUINEA

GABON

SAO TOME AND PRINCIPE

CONGO

ANGOL

NAMI

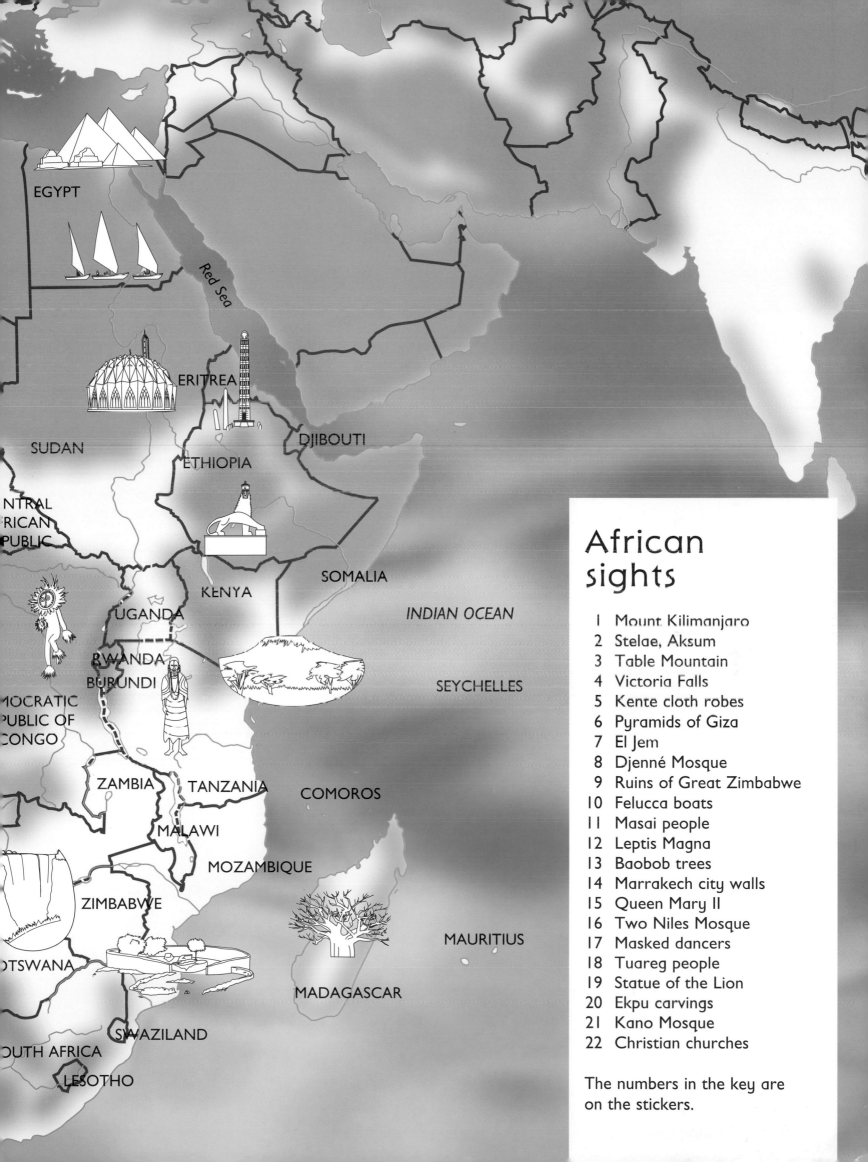

EGYPT

Red Sea

ERITREA

SUDAN

DJIBOUTI

ETHIOPIA

CENTRAL
AFRICAN
REPUBLIC

SOMALIA

KENYA

INDIAN OCEAN

UGANDA

RWANDA

BURUNDI

DEMOCRATIC
REPUBLIC OF
CONGO

SEYCHELLES

ZAMBIA

TANZANIA

COMOROS

MALAWI

MOZAMBIQUE

ZIMBABWE

MAURITIUS

BOTSWANA

MADAGASCAR

SWAZILAND

SOUTH AFRICA

LESOTHO

# African sights

1   Mount Kilimanjaro
2   Stelae, Aksum
3   Table Mountain
4   Victoria Falls
5   Kente cloth robes
6   Pyramids of Giza
7   El Jem
8   Djenné Mosque
9   Ruins of Great Zimbabwe
10  Felucca boats
11  Masai people
12  Leptis Magna
13  Baobob trees
14  Marrakech city walls
15  Queen Mary II
16  Two Niles Mosque
17  Masked dancers
18  Tuareg people
19  Statue of the Lion
20  Ekpu carvings
21  Kano Mosque
22  Christian churches

The numbers in the key are
on the stickers.

# Asia

RUSSIA

Black Sea

Caspian
Sea

Mediterranean
Sea

KAZAKHSTAN

UZBEKISTAN

TURKMENISTAN

KYRGYZSTAN

TAJIKISTAN

CHINA

AFGHANISTAN

PAKISTAN

NEPAL BHUTAN

BANGLADESH

BURMA
(MYANMA...

Red
Sea

Arabian
Sea

INDIA

Bay of
Bengal

SRI LANKA

MALDIVES

INDIAN OCEAN

Bering Sea

Sea of
Okhotsk

Sea of
Japan

NORTH
KOREA

SOUTH
KOREA

JAPAN

MONGOLIA

Taiwan

VIETNAM

OS

AILAND

AMBODIA

South
China Sea

PHILIPPINES

Philippine
Sea

PACIFIC
OCEAN

BRUNEI

ALAYSIA

GAPORE

Borneo

Celebes

umatra

INDONESIA

New Guinea

Java

EAST
TIMOR

# Asian sights

23 Mount Everest
24 Torii gate
25 Great Wall of China
26 Giant Buddha, Leshan
27 Forbidden City
28 Shwedagon Pagoda
29 Angkor Wat
30 Painted elephants
31 Floating markets
32 Terracotta Army
33 Borobudur Temple
34 Mount Fuji
35 Golden Temple, Amritsar
36 Steppe herders
37 Taj Mahal
38 Banaue rice terraces
39 Sigiriya Rock Fortress
40 Trans-Siberian Railway
41 Bharatnatyam dancers
42 Taipei 101 Tower
43 Baikonur space station
44 Yurts
45 Blue Mosque,
   Mazar-e Sharif
46 Icebreaker ships

The numbers in the key are
on the stickers.

7

# North and Central America

ARCTIC OCEAN

GREENLAND
(Denmark)

Ellesmere
Island

Queen Elizabeth
Islands

Baffin
Bay

Baffin
Island

Labrador
Sea

Newfoundland

ATLANTIC
OCEAN

Hudson
Bay

Victoria
Island

Beaufort
Sea

CANADA

The Great

ALASKA (USA)

Gulf of
Alaska

PACIFIC
OCEAN

# North and Central American sights

47 Grand Canyon
48 Niagara Falls
49 Day of the Dead festival
50 Mount McKinley
51 Mississippi paddle boats
52 Giant redwood trees
53 CN Tower
54 Panama Canal
55 Totem poles
56 Pueblo de Taos
57 Statue of Liberty
58 Kennedy Space Center
59 Mount Rushmore
60 Chichen Itza
61 Hollywood
62 Gateway Arch
63 Seattle Space Needle
64 Calgary stampede
65 Old Havana Cathedral
66 White House
67 Inuit people
68 Mayan temple, Tikal
69 Golden Gate Bridge
70 Ice hockey players

The numbers in the key are on the stickers.

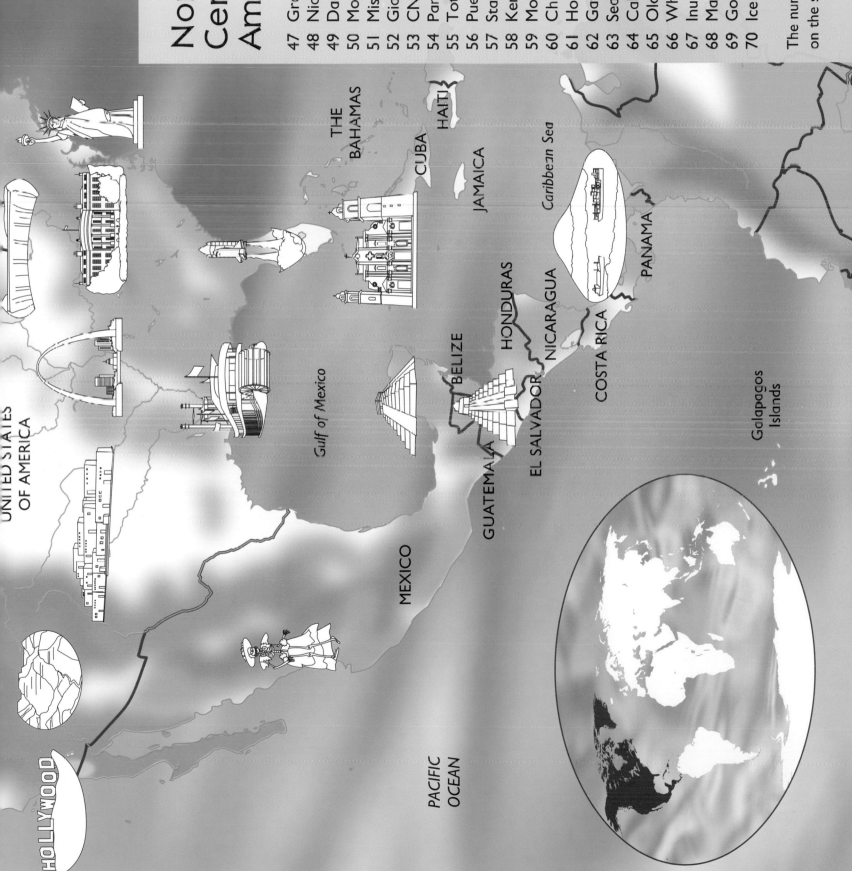

UNITED STATES OF AMERICA

HOLLYWOOD

PACIFIC OCEAN

MEXICO

Gulf of Mexico

THE BAHAMAS

CUBA

HAITI

JAMAICA

Caribbean Sea

GUATEMALA

BELIZE

HONDURAS

EL SALVADOR

NICARAGUA

COSTA RICA

PANAMA

Galapagos Islands

9

# South America

*Caribbean Sea*

ATLANTIC
OCEAN

VENEZUELA

GUYANA

SURINAM

FRENCH
GUIANA
(France)

COLOMBIA

BRAZIL

ECUADOR

PERU

BOLIVIA

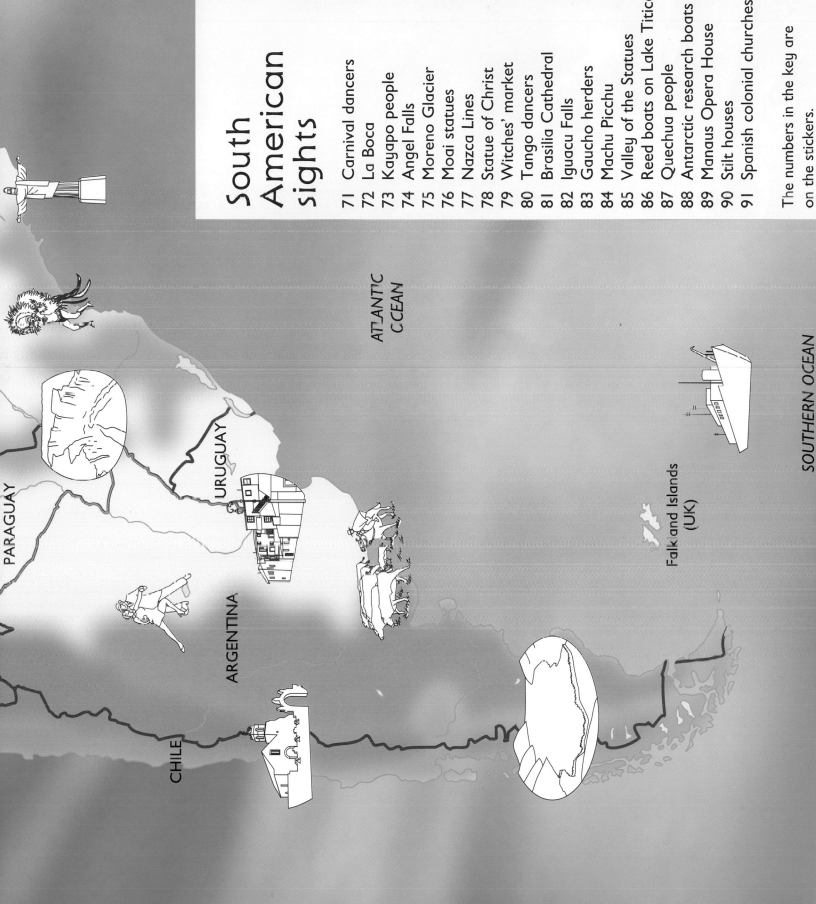

# South American sights

71 Carnival dancers
72 La Boca
73 Kayapo people
74 Angel Falls
75 Moreno Glacier
76 Moai statues
77 Nazca Lines
78 Statue of Christ
79 Witches' market
80 Tango dancers
81 Brasilia Cathedral
82 Iguacu Falls
83 Gaucho herders
84 Machu Picchu
85 Valley of the Statues
86 Reed boats on Lake Titicaca
87 Quechua people
88 Antarctic research boats
89 Manaus Opera House
90 Stilt houses
91 Spanish colonial churches

The numbers in the key are on the stickers.

PARAGUAY

URUGUAY

ARGENTINA

CHILE

PACIFIC OCEAN

ATLANTIC OCEAN

Falkland Islands (UK)

SOUTHERN OCEAN

Easter Island is 2,300 miles (3,700 km) from the coast of Chile.

# The Middle East

GEORGIA

ARMENIA

AZERBAIJAN

TURKEY

*Mediterranean Sea*

IRAQ

LEBANON

SYRIA

JORDAN

ISRAEL

*Red Sea*

IRAN

KUWAIT

BAHRAIN

SAUDI ARABIA

QATAR

UNITED ARAB EMIRATES

OMAN

YEMEN

*Arabian Sea*

Socotra (Yemen)

*INDIAN OCEAN*

## Middle Eastern sights

92   Bin Ali Mosque
93   Blue Mosque, Istanbul
94   Ziggurat temple
95   Aleppo Citadel
96   Western Wall and Dome of the Rock
97   Modern hotels
98   Throne hall, Persepolis
99   Emam Mosque
100  Grand Mosque, Mecca
101  Cappadocia caves
102  Petra
103  Sana old town

The numbers in the key are on the stickers.

58

30

42

20

139

125

91

107

43

52

106

67

73

121

109

45

130

40

115

16

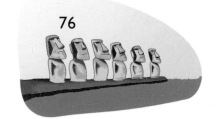
76

105

88

68

5

80

86

46

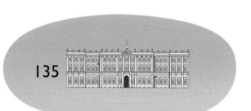

118

95

94

128

13

137

61

HOLLYWOOD

104

135

49

83

11

77

143

38

23

15

1

96

92

62

113

 85

 27

 97

 84

 54

 63

 26

 141

 6

 32

 120

 18

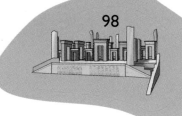 98

 66

 14

 112

 48

 138

 87

 55

 100

 8

 51

 39

 50

 126

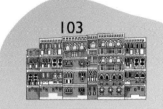 103

 114

 74

 57

 136

 10

 117

 134

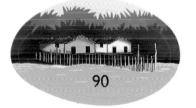 90

 41

 21

 34

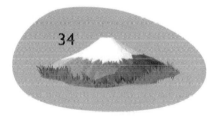 99

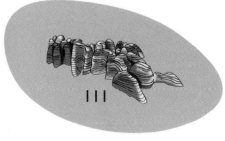 111

 119

 12

 44

 7

 89

 24

 29

 69

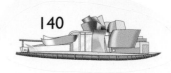 140

 3

129

 33

 47

 133

 101

 142

 4

 28

78

 65

 144

 9

 81

 31

 124

 93

 59

 102

 79

 22

 18

53

64

19

108

132

37

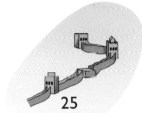
25

56

82

122

17

131

116

127

75

36

70

71

123

110

72

2

35

60

# Australasia

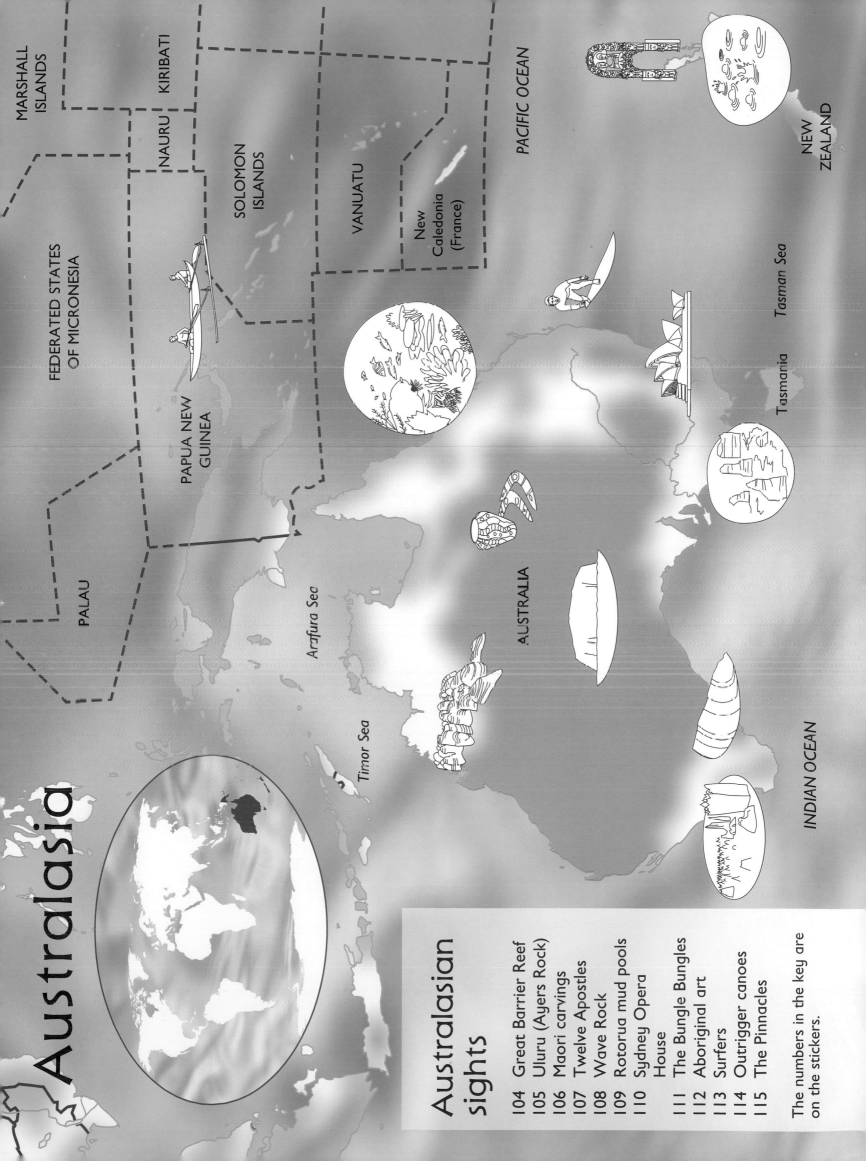

MARSHALL ISLANDS

NAURU  KIRIBATI

FEDERATED STATES OF MICRONESIA

PALAU

SOLOMON ISLANDS

PAPUA NEW GUINEA

VANUATU

New Caledonia (France)

*PACIFIC OCEAN*

NEW ZEALAND

*Tasman Sea*

Tasmania

AUSTRALIA

*Arafura Sea*

*Timor Sea*

*INDIAN OCEAN*

## Australasian sights

104  Great Barrier Reef
105  Uluru (Ayers Rock)
106  Maori carvings
107  Twelve Apostles
108  Wave Rock
109  Rotorua mud pools
110  Sydney Opera House
111  The Bungle Bungles
112  Aboriginal art
113  Surfers
114  Outrigger canoes
115  The Pinnacles

The numbers in the key are on the stickers.

# Europe

ICELAND

*Norwegian Sea*

NORWAY

SWED

IRELAND

UNITED KINGDOM

*North Sea*

DENMARK

ATLANTIC OCEAN

NETHERLANDS

BELGIUM

GERMANY

CZEC
REPUBL

*Bay of Biscay*

FRANCE

SWITZERLAND

AUSTRI

SLOVEN

CROAT

SPAIN

PORTUGAL

ITALY

Corsica

Sardinia

*Mediterranean Sea*

Sicily

MALTA

14

Barents Sea

FINLAND

RUSSIA

ESTONIA

LATVIA

altic
ea

LITHUANIA

BELARUS

OLAND

UKRAINE

LOVAKIA

MOLDOVA

NGARY

ROMANIA

INA

SERBIA

Black Sea

GRO   KOSOVO

BULGARIA

MACEDONIA

TURKEY

ALBANIA

GREECE   Aegean
Sea

CYPRUS

Crete

# European sights

116 Ballet dancers
117 Strokkur geyser
118 Olavinlinna Castle
119 Giant's Causeway
120 Bran Castle
121 Belem Tower
122 Ice hotel
123 Neuschwanstein Castle
124 St. Basil's Cathedral
125 The Colosseum
126 Wooden churches
127 Eiffel Tower
128 Palace of Westminster
129 Celtic crosses
130 The Little Mermaid
131 Church of the
    Sagrada Familia
132 The Parthenon
133 Malbork Castle
134 Mount Etna
135 Winter Palace
136 Mont St. Michel
137 Tyn Church
138 Sami people
139 Leaning Tower of Pisa
140 Guggenheim Museum,
    Bilbao
141 Edinburgh Castle
142 Flamenco dancers
143 Cossack dancers
144 Minoan palace

The numbers in the key are
on the stickers.

# Flags of the world

These pages show the flags of the world's 194 independent states. The name of the state and its capital city are given below each flag.

## Africa

**Morocco**
Rabat

**Algeria**
Algiers

**Tunisia**
Tunis

**Libya**
Tripoli

**Egypt**
Cairo

**Mauritania**
Nouakchott

**Mali**
Bamako

**Niger**
Niamey

**Chad**
N'Djamena

**Sudan**
Khartoum

**Eritrea**
Asmara

**Ethiopia**
Addis Ababa

**Djibouti**
Djibouti

**Somalia**
Mogadishu

**Cape Verde**
Praia

**Senegal**
Dakar

**The Gambia**
Banjul

**Guinea-Bissau**
Bissau

**Guinea**
Conakry

**Sierra Leone**
Freetown

**Liberia**
Monrovia

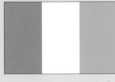
**Ivory Coast**
Yamoussoukro

**Burkina Faso**
Ouagadougou

**Ghana**
Accra

**Togo**
Lome

**Benin**
Porto-Novo

**Nigeria**
Abuja

**Cameroon**
Yaounde

**Central African Republic**
Bangui

**Equatorial Guinea**
Malabo

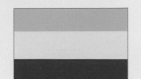

**Sao Tome and Principe**
Sao Tome

**Gabon**
Libreville

**Congo**
Brazzaville

**Democratic Republic of the Congo**
Kinshasa

**Uganda**
Kampala

**Kenya**
Nairobi

**Seychelles**
Victoria

**Rwanda**
Kigali

**Burundi**
Bujumbura

**Tanzania**
Dar es Salaam, Dodoma

**Angola**
Luanda

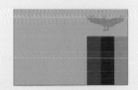

**Zambia**
Lusaka

**Malawi**
Lilongwe

**Mozambique**
Maputo

**Zimbabwe**
Harare

**Comoros**
Moroni

**Madagascar**
Antananarivo

**Mauritius**
Port Louis

**Namibia**
Windhoek

**Botswana**
Gaborone

**South Africa**
Pretoria, Cape Town, Bloemfontein

**Lesotho**
Maseru

**Swaziland**
Mbabane, Lobamba

# Asia

**Russia**
Moscow

**Georgia**
Tbilisi

**Armenia**
Yerevan

**Azerbaijan**
Baku

**Kazakhstan**
Astana

**Uzbekistan**
Tashkent

**Turkmenistan**
Ashgabat (Ashkhabad)

**Tajikistan**
Dushanbe

**Kyrgyzstan**
Bishkek

**China**
Beijing

# Asia (continued)

**Mongolia**
Ulan Bator

**North Korea**
Pyongyang

**South Korea**
Seoul

**Japan**
Tokyo

**Afghanistan**
Kabul

**Pakistan**
Islamabad

**India**
New Delhi

**Nepal**
Kathmandu

**Bhutan**
Thimphu

**Bangladesh**
Dhaka

**Burma (Myanmar)**
Rangoon, Naypyidaw

**Thailand**
Bangkok

**Laos**
Vientiane

**Cambodia**
Phnom Penh

**Vietnam**
Hanoi

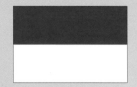

**Philippines**
Manila

**Maldives**
Male

**Sri Lanka**
Colombo, Sri
Jayewardenepura Kotte

**Malaysia**
Kuala Lumpur

**Singapore**
Singapore

**Brunei**
Bandar Seri Begawan

**Indonesia**
Jakarta

**East Timor**
Dili

# North and Central America

**Canada**
Ottawa

**United States
of America**
Washington DC

**Mexico**
Mexico City

**Guatemala**
Guatemala City

**Belize**
Belmopan

**El Salvador**
San Salvador

**Honduras**
Tegucigalpa

**Nicaragua**
Managua

**Costa Rica**
San Jose

**Panama**
Panama City

# North and Central America (continued)

**The Bahamas**
Nassau

**Cuba**
Havana

**Jamaica**
Kingston

**Haiti**
Port-au-Prince

**Dominican Republic**
Santo Domingo

**Saint Kitts and Nevis**
Basseterre

**Antigua and Barbuda**
Saint John's

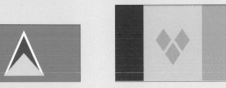
**Dominica**
Roseau

**Saint Lucia**
Castries

**Saint Vincent and the Grenadines**
Kingstown

**Barbados**
Bridgetown

**Grenada**
Saint George's

**Trinidad and Tobago**
Port-of-Spain

# South America

**Colombia**
Bogota

**Venezuela**
Caracas

**Guyana**
Georgetown

**Suriname**
Paramaribo

**Ecuador**
Quito

**Peru**
Lima

**Brazil**
Brasilia

**Bolivia**
La Paz, Sucre

**Paraguay**
Asuncion

**Chile**
Santiago

**Argentina**
Buenos Aires

**Uruguay**
Montevideo

# The Middle East

**Turkey**
Ankara

**Syria**
Damascus

**Iraq**
Baghdad

**Iran**
Tehran

**Lebanon**
Beirut

# The Middle East (continued)

**Israel**
Jerusalem

**Jordan**
Amman

**Saudi Arabia**
Riyadh

**Kuwait**
Kuwait City

**Bahrain**
Manama

**Qatar**
Doha

**United Arab Emirates**
Abu Dhabi

**Oman**
Muscat

**Yemen**
Sana

# Australasia and Oceania

**Palau**
Melekeok

**Federated States of Micronesia**
Palikir

**Marshall Islands**
Majuro

**Papua New Guinea**
Port Moresby

**Nauru**
Yaren

**Kiribati**
Bairiki (on Tarawa island)

**Solomon Islands**
Honiara

**Tuvalu**
Funafuti

**Samoa**
Apia

**Australia**
Canberra

**Vanuatu**
Port-Vila

**Fiji**
Suva

**Tonga**
Nukualofa

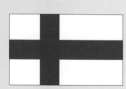
**New Zealand**
Wellington

# Europe

**Iceland**
Reykjavik

**Norway**
Oslo

**Sweden**
Stockholm

**Finland**
Helsinki

**Ireland**
Dublin

**United Kingdom**
London

**Netherlands**
Amsterdam, The Hague

**Belgium**
Brussels

**Luxembourg**
Luxembourg

**Germany**
Berlin

# Europe (continued)

 **Denmark**
Copenhagen

 **Poland**
Warsaw

 **Lithuania**
Vilnius

 **Latvia**
Riga

 **Estonia**
Tallinn

 **Belarus**
Minsk

 **Czech Republic**
Prague

 **Slovakia**
Bratislava

 **Ukraine**
Kiev

 **France**
Paris

 **Switzerland**
Bern

 **Liechtenstein**
Vaduz

 **Austria**
Vienna

 **Hungary**
Budapest

 **Romania**
Bucharest

 **Moldova**
Chisinau

 **Portugal**
Lisbon

 **Spain**
Madrid

 **Andorra**
Andorra la Vella

 **Monaco**
Monaco

 **Italy**
Rome

 **San Marino**
San Marino

 **Vatican City**
Vatican City

 **Slovenia**
Ljubljana

 **Croatia**
Zagreb

 **Bosnia and
Herzegovina**
Sarajevo

 **Serbia**
Belgrade

 **Albania**
Tirana

 **Macedonia**
Skopje

 **Bulgaria**
Sofia

 **Greece**
Athens

 **Malta**
Valletta

 **Cyprus**
Nicosia

 **Montenegro**
Podgorica

 **Kosovo**
Pristina

# World records

Here are some of the world's longest rivers, tallest buildings, highest mountains and other incredible world records.

## The highest mountains

- Everest, Nepal/China   8,850m   (29,035ft)
- K2, Pakistan/China   8,611m   (28,251ft)
- Kanchenjunga, India/Nepal   8,597m   (28,208ft)
- Lhotse I, Nepal/China   8,511m   (27,923ft)
- Makalu I, Nepal/China   8,481m   (27,824ft)
- Lhotse II, Nepal/China   8,400m   (27,560ft)
- Dhaulagiri, Nepal   8,172m   (26,810ft)
- Manaslu I, Nepal   8,156m   (26,760ft)
- Cho Oyu, Nepal/China   8,153m   (26,750ft)
- Nanga Parbat, Pakistan   8,126m   (26,660ft)

### Mountain ranges

The world's longest mountain range is the Andes, which stretches along the west of South America from Venezuela to the southern tip of Chile. The highest range is the Himalayas, in Asia, which is where Mount Everest is.

## Longest rivers

- Nile, Africa   6,671km   (4,145 miles)
- Amazon, South America   6,440km   (4,000 miles)
- Chang Jiang (Yangtze), China   6,380km   (3,964 miles)
- Mississippi/Missouri, USA   6,019km   (3,741 miles)
- Yenisey/Angara, Russia   5,540km   (3,442 miles)
- Huang He (Yellow), China   5,464km   (3,395 miles)
- Ob/Irtysh/Black Irtysh, Asia   5,411km   (3,362 miles)
- Amur/Shilka/Onon, Asia   4,416km   (2,744 miles)
- Lena, Russia   4,400km   (2,734 miles)
- Congo, Africa   4,374km   (2,718 miles)

### Wet and dry

The Amazon Rainforest, in South America, is the wettest place in the world. The driest place is the Atacama Desert, also in South America, where it has rained only a few times in the last 400 years.

## Famous waterfalls

- Angel Falls, Venezuela   979m   (3,212ft)
- Sutherland Falls, New Zealand   580m   (1,904ft)
- Mardalfossen, Norway   517m   (1,696ft)
- Jog Falls, India   253m   (830ft)
- Victoria Falls, Zimbabwe/Zambia   108m   (355ft)
- Iguacu Falls, Brazil/Argentina   82m   (269ft)
- Niagara Falls, Canada/USA   57m   (187ft)

### Naming Angel Falls

Angel Falls were discovered in 1935. They were named after James Angel, an American who crashed his plane near them in 1937.

# Biggest natural lakes

- Caspian Sea       370,999 sq km    (143,243 sq miles)
- Lake Superior       82,414 sq km     (31,820 sq miles)
- Lake Victoria       69,215 sq km     (26,724 sq miles)
- Lake Huron       59,596 sq km     (23,010 sq miles)
- Lake Michigan       58,016 sq km     (22,400 sq miles)
- Lake Tanganyika    32,764 sq km     (12,650 sq miles)
- Lake Baikal       31,500 sq km     (12,162 sq miles)
- Great Bear Lake    31,328 sq km     (12,096 sq miles)
- Lake Nyasa       29,928 sq km     (11,555 sq miles)
- Aral Sea       28,600 sq km     (11,042 sq miles)

## Deep water

The deepest lake in the world is Russia's Lake Baikal. It is 1,642m (5,387ft) deep. The deepest part of the sea is the Pacific Ocean's Mariana Trench, which is up to 11,022m (36,161ft) deep.

# Biggest islands

- Greenland       2,175,600 sq km    (840,000 sq miles)
- New Guinea       800,000 sq km    (309,000 sq miles)
- Borneo       751,100 sq km    (290,000 sq miles)
- Madagascar       587,040 sq km    (226,656 sq miles)
- Baffin Island       507,451 sq km    (195,928 sq miles)
- Sumatra       437,607 sq km    (184,706 sq miles)
- Great Britain       234,410 sq km    (90,506 sq miles)
- Honshu       227,920 sq km    (88,000 sq miles)
- Victoria Island       217,290 sq km    (83,896 sq miles)
- Ellesmere Island    196,236 sq km    (75,767 sq miles)

## Big and small

The biggest country in the world is Russia, which covers an area of 17,075,200 sq km (6,592,735 sq miles). The smallest is the Vatican City, which measures only 0.44 sq km (0.17 sq miles).

# Tallest inhabited buildings

- Taipei 101 Tower, Taiwan    508m    (1,674ft)
- Petronas Towers, Malaysia    452m    (1,483ft)
- Sears Tower, USA    443m    (1,454ft)
- Jin Mao Building, China    420m    (1,378ft)
- Two International Finance Centre, Hong Kong    412m    (1,350ft)
- CITIC Plaza, China    391m    (1,283ft)
- Shun Hing Square, China    384m    (1,260ft)
- Plaza Rakyat, Malaysia    382m    (1,254ft)
- Empire State Building, USA    381m    (1,250ft)
- Central Plaza, China    373m    (1,227ft)

## Crowded places

The least populated country is the Vatican City, where only around 900 people live. The most populated is China, with a population of over 1,280,000,000. A third of the people in the world live in China and India.

# Index and checklist

This checklist will help you to find the sights in the book. The first number after each entry tells you which page it is on. The second number is the number on the sticker.

Aboriginal art, 13 (112)
Aleppo Citadel, 12 (95)
Angel Falls, 10 (74)
Angkor Wat, 7 (29)
Antarctic research boats, 11 (88)

Baikonur space station, 6 (43)
Ballet dancers, 15 (116)
Banaue rice terraces, 7 (38)
Baobob trees, 5 (13)
Belem Tower, 14 (121)
Bharatnatyam dancers, 6 (41)
Bin Ali Mosque, 12 (92)
Blue Mosque, Istanbul, 12 (93)
Blue Mosque, Mazar-e Sharif, 6 (45)
Boca, La, 11 (72)
Borobudur Temple, 7 (33)
Bran Castle, 15 (120)
Brasilia Cathedral, 10 (81)
Bungle Bungles, the, 13 (111)

Calgary stampede, 8 (64)
Cappadocia caves, 12 (101)
Carnival dancers, 11 (71)
Celtic crosses, 14 (129)
Chichen Itza, 9 (60)
Christian churches, 4 (22)
Church of the Sagrada Familia, 14 (131)
CN Tower, 8 (53)
Colosseum, the, 14 (125)
Cossack dancers, 15 (143)

Day of the Dead festival, 9 (49)
Djenné Mosque, 4 (8)

Edinburgh Castle, 14 (141)
Eiffel Tower, 14 (127)
Ekpu carvings, 4 (20)
El Jem, 4 (7)
Emam Mosque, 12 (99)

Felucca boats, 5 (10)
Flamenco dancers, 14 (142)
Floating markets, 7 (31)
Forbidden City, 7 (27)

Gateway Arch, 9 (62)
Gaucho herders, 11 (83)
Giant Buddha, Leshan, 7 (26)
Giant redwood trees, 8 (52)
Giant's Causeway, 14 (119)
Golden Gate Bridge, 8 (69)
Golden Temple, Amritsar, 6 (35)
Grand Canyon, 9 (47)
Grand Mosque, Mecca, 12 (100)
Great Barrier Reef, 13 (104)
Great Wall of China, 7 (25)
Guggenheim Museum, Bilbao, 14 (140)

Hollywood, 9 (61)

Icebreaker ships, 7 (46)
Ice hockey players, 8 (70)
Ice hotel, 15 (122)
Iguacu Falls, 11 (82)
Inuit people, 8 (67)

Kano Mosque, 4 (21)
Kayapo people, 10 (73)

Kennedy Space Center, 9 (58)
Kente cloth robes, 4 (5)

Leaning Tower of Pisa, 14 (139)
Leptis Magna, 4 (12)
Little Mermaid, the, 14 (130)

Machu Picchu, 10 (84)
Malbork Castle, 15 (133)
Manaus Opera House, 10 (89)
Maori carvings, 13 (106)
Marrakech city walls, 4 (14)
Masai people, 5 (11)
Masked dancers, 5 (17)
Mayan temple, Tikal, 9 (68)
Minoan palace, 15 (144)
Mississippi paddle boats, 9 (51)
Moai statues, 11 (76)
Modern hotels, 12 (97)
Mont St. Michel, 14 (136)
Moreno Glacier, 11 (75)
Mount Etna, 14 (134)
Mount Everest, 6 (23)
Mount Fuji, 7 (34)
Mount Kilimanjaro, 5 (1)
Mount McKinley, 8 (50)
Mount Rushmore, 8 (59)

Nazca Lines, 10 (77)
Neuschwanstein Castle, 14 (123)
Niagara Falls, 9 (48)

Olavinlinna Castle, 15 (118)
Old Havana Cathedral, 9 (65)

Outrigger canoes, 13 (114)

Painted elephants, 6 (30)
Palace of Westminster, 14 (128)
Panama Canal, 9 (54)
Parthenon, the, 15 (132)
Petra, 12 (102)
Pinnacles, the, 13 (115)
Pueblo de Taos, 9 (56)
Pyramids of Giza, 5 (6)

Quechua people, 10 (87)
Queen Mary II, 4 (15)

Reed boats on Lake Titicaca, 10 (86)
Rotorua mud pools, 13 (109)
Ruins of Great Zimbabwe, 5 (9)

St. Basil's Cathedral, 15 (124)
Sami people, 15 (138)
Sana old town, 12 (103)
Seattle Space Needle, 8 (63)
Shwedagon Pagoda, 6 (28)
Sigiriya Rock Fortress, 6 (39)
Spanish colonial churches, 11 (91)
Statue of Christ, 11 (78)
Statue of Liberty, 9 (57)
Statue of the Lion, 5 (19)
Stelae, Aksum, 5 (2)
Steppe herders, 6 (36)
Stilt houses, 10 (90)
Strokkur geyser, 14 (117)
Surfers, 13 (113)
Sydney Opera House, 13 (110)

Table Mountain, 4 (3)
Taipei 101 Tower, 7 (42)
Taj Mahal, 6 (37)
Tango dancers, 11 (80)
Terracotta Army, 7 (32)
Throne hall, Persepolis, 12 (98)
Torii gate, 7 (24)
Totem poles, 8 (55)
Trans-Siberian Railway, 6 (40)
Tuareg people, 4 (18)
Twelve Apostles, 13 (107)
Two Niles Mosque, 5 (16)
Tyn Church, 14 (137)

Uluru (Ayers Rock), 13 (105)

Valley of the Statues, 10 (85)
Victoria Falls, 5 (4)

Wave Rock, 13 (108)
Western Wall and Dome of the Rock, 12 (96)
White House, 9 (66)
Winter Palace, 15 (135)
Witches' market, 10 (79)
Wooden churches, 14 (126)

Yurts, 7 (44)

Ziggurat temple, 12 (94)

Additional design by Kate Fearn and Neil Francis
Editorial assistance by Rachel Firth and Leonie Pratt
Cartographer: Craig Asquith
Flags consultant: Jos Poels
Flag images by worldflagpictures.com